First published in the United States, Great Britain, Canada,
Australia, and New Zealand in 2000 by North-South Books,
an imprint of Nord-Süd Verlag AG, Gossau Zürich, Switzerland.

Distributed in the United States by North-South Books Inc., New York.

Library of Congress Cataloging-in-Publication Data is available.
A CIP catalogue record for this book is available from The British Library.
ISBN 0-7358-1340-X (trade binding) 10 9 8 7 6 5 4 3 2 1
ISBN 0-7358-1341-8 (library binding) 10 9 8 7 6 5 4 3 2 1
Printed in Germany

For more information about our books, and the authors and artists
who create them, visit our web site: www.northsouth.com

A Michael Neugebauer Book
NORTH-SOUTH BOOKS / NEW YORK / LONDON

THE EMPEROR'S NEW CLOTHES

By Hans Christian Andersen
Adapted and Illustrated by Eve Tharlet
Translated by Rosemary Lanning

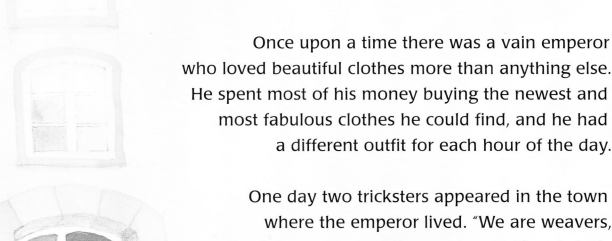

Once upon a time there was a vain emperor who loved beautiful clothes more than anything else. He spent most of his money buying the newest and most fabulous clothes he could find, and he had a different outfit for each hour of the day.

One day two tricksters appeared in the town where the emperor lived. "We are weavers, and we can weave the most magnificent cloth you have ever seen," they told the astonished townspeople. "Our cloth is truly remarkable," they went on. "For it is invisible to stupid people or those who are not good at their jobs."

When the emperor heard about the amazing cloth,
he was very excited. What splendid clothes could be
made from that cloth! he thought. Why, with such cloth
I could see at once who is not good at his job and who
is clever and who is stupid.
He sent for the two weavers, gave them a great deal
of gold for some of the wonderful cloth, and told them
to start work immediately.
The two tricksters demanded silk and special thread
and precious stones to weave into the emperor's
new clothes. They set up their looms
and pretended to weave.

Every morning the emperor's first thought
was for the new clothes.
"I would like to know what the cloth looks like,"
he said to himself. "But suppose I could not see it
at all? That would mean I was stupid or not a
good emperor! No, first I will send my trusted
old minister. He will tell me how
the work is progressing."

So the trusted old minister went into
the weavers' workshop, where the two tricksters
sat at their empty looms.
"Step closer, Minister, sir!" cried the tricksters.
"See how beautiful the cloth is!"
The old minister's eyes widened in shock.
He could see nothing, nothing at all!
Good heavens! he thought, horrified.
Am I stupid? Or am I not a good minister?
No one must ever hear of this!
"Well," asked the tricksters, "how do you like it?"
"Oh, it is superb, quite lovely," the old minister lied.
"I will report to the emperor that I am
very pleased with it."

The two weavers demanded more silk, gold,
and precious stones for the emperor's new clothes.
They put everything in their own pockets and
went on working at the empty looms.
Soon the emperor sent his most loyal footman
to the weavers to find out when the cloth would be
ready. But things went exactly the same way for
the footman as they had for the minister.
He stared until his eyes nearly popped out of his
head—but all he saw were the two empty looms.
Does this mean I am stupid or not a good footman?
he thought. I must not let anyone find out!
So the footman praised the beautiful cloth and
told the emperor that it was truly splendid.

Everyone in the town was talking of nothing but the fabulous cloth. And by now the emperor was so curious he wanted to see it himself. He chose some of the most clever people in his court to come with him, including the old minister and the footman. Together they went into the tricksters' workshop, where the two men clattered busily at the empty looms.

"See, Your Majesty, isn't it gorgeous?"
asked the minister and the footman. They
pointed to the empty loom, believing that
everyone else could see the beautiful cloth.
The emperor turned pale.
What's this? he thought, horrified.
I see nothing at all! Does this mean I am stupid
or useless as an emperor? That would be the
most terrible thing that could happen to me.
No one must find out!
"Oh, it's very pretty!" cried the emperor.
"I am extremely pleased!"
His companions nodded in agreement.
They couldn't see a single thread either,
but no one dared admit it.
"Yes, it is charming, splendid, wonderful,"
they all said.
"Your Majesty, you should wear new clothes
made from this magnificent cloth in the
great procession," declared the old minister.
The emperor agreed, and asked the two tricksters
to make a ceremonial outfit from the cloth.

The tricksters worked day and night.
Everyone saw how busy they were.
They lifted the cloth from the looms,
they snipped away with large scissors,
they stitched and fitted, they sewed
with needles without any thread,
and at last they said:
"The emperor's new clothes are ready!"

The two tricksters carried the new clothes
into the emperor's dressing room. They lifted
their arms in the air and said, "Here are the
trousers! Here is the jacket! Just look at this
cloak! All the clothes are as light as spiders'
webs. You will feel as if you had nothing
on at all, but that is what is so special
about them."
They both pretended to dress the emperor
in the new clothes. They smoothed out creases,
buttoned his waistcoat, and fastened the long
train. And the emperor twisted and turned in
front of the mirror, pretending to admire
the new clothes.
"Oh, what a truly magnificent suit!" cried the
courtiers eagerly, although none of them
could see anything.
At last the emperor was ready.

The footmen held out their arms stiffly in front of them as if
they were carrying the emperor's train. They didn't want anyone
to notice that they could not see the cloak.
The emperor strode out of the castle gate proudly. Servants were
already waiting there with a canopy. The procession began.

The people in the streets clapped
when they saw the emperor.
"Oh, just look at those wonderful clothes!"
they all cried as the emperor marched down
the streets in his underwear, waving cheerfully.
Nobody wanted to admit that they couldn't see
anything because they didn't want
to appear stupid.

Suddenly a child called out: "But the emperor has nothing on at all!"
"Did you hear that?" said an old man. "The child is telling the truth."
And one person whispered to another: "The emperor has nothing on at all! He has nothing on at all!"

Soon everyone was laughing at the emperor's new clothes.
The emperor was very embarrassed, for he knew that they were right.
All I can do is carry on, he thought, and grimly continued strutting through the town. And his servants went on carrying the train that was not there.
As for the two tricksters, they hurried off with the foolish emperor's gold and were never seen again.